HOLY MOLÉ!

A folktale from Mexico

Caroline McAlister
Illustrated by Stefan Czernecki

AUGUST HOUSE
LittleFolk

ATLANTA

To my mother, Judith McAlister,
who took me to the Mexican folk art exhibit
and has encouraged my writing all along.—CM

To my friend Eiji Iriguchi.—SC

Published 2007 by August House Publishers, Inc.
3500 Piedmont Road, Suite 310
Atlanta, GA 30305
404-442-4420
http://www.augusthouse.com

Book design by Doug McCaffry

Manufactured in Korea

10 9 8 7 6 5 4 3 2 1

LIBRARY OF CONGRESS CATALOGING-IN-PUBLICATION DATA
McAlister, Caroline, 1960-
Holy Molé! : a folktale from Mexico / Caroline McAlister; illustrations by Stefan Czernecki.
p.   cm.
Summary: A retelling of the traditional Mexican tale explaining the origins of molé,
the savory chocolate sauce that is served over turkey or chicken.
Includes bibliographical references.
ISBN-13: 978-0-87483-775-9 (hardcover : alk. paper)
ISBN-10: 0-87483-775-8 (hardcover : alk. paper)
[1. Folklore—Mexico. 2. Cookery, Mexican—Folklore] I. Czernecki, Stefan, ill. II. Title
PZ8.1.M117Ho2007
398.2—dc22

[E]   2006040726

The paper used in this publication meets the minimum requirements of the
American National Standard for Information Sciences—
Permanence of Paper for Printed Library Materials,
ANSI Z39.48-1984.

AUGUST HOUSE PUBLISHERS ATLANTA

Carlos squatted under the kitchen table
as he cleaned the monastery floor.

He heard someone enter the room.

Carlos saw the cook, Brother Pascual, followed closely by Bishop Roberto.

Brother Pascual was wringing his hands. "The Viceroy is coming to visit!" he exclaimed. "What will we feed him? He is used to the finest meals. We are simple people."

"I am sure you will think of something," Bishop Roberto replied. "See to it that everything is ready by noon."

"Noon! We have just two hours before he arrives?"
Brother Pascual began to give orders.

"You, grind the corn for the tortillas.
"You, light the fire.
"You, chop some chilies for the sauce.
"You, pluck those turkeys, and be careful.
The Viceroy does not like turkey feathers
in his stew."

"And you, Carlos, little kitchen boy, help Brother Juan with the tortillas."

"But who is this Viceroy?" asked Carlos.

"The most important man in the colony of Mexico! He tells the king of Spain everything that happens here. We must make a good impression."

"And what if we don't impress him?" Carlos asked.

"No more questions! And when the Viceroy arrives, stay out of sight. Once His Honor leaves, you can have something to eat yourself."

As he patted the cornmeal into tortillas, Carlos wondered how he could help the brothers impress the Viceroy. He was only an orphan boy who worked in the kitchen for scraps of food. He thought about his empty stomach as he watched the brothers work.

They cut. They sliced. They plucked.
They baked. They boiled.

The bells rang eleven times, and still they were not ready.

"Hurry, hurry," said Brother Pascual.
"We don't want the Viceroy to sit
down to an empty table."

They kneaded. They ground. They mashed.
They simmered. They fried.

The brothers worked fast.

"Brother Pascual, here are cinnamon and chocolate for the dessert. Hmmm! Smell them!"

"Here are the chilies for the salsa. Ooh! They are hot and tasty!"

"And here is the onion for the stew. Take it quickly before I start crying."

Brother Pascual rushed from one end of the kitchen to the other with a large tray. He gathered ingredients for five different sauces and two desserts.

Carlos had finished patting out the tortillas. He was waiting to sneak a bite of something sweet. Across the room he spied a raisin bun that had fallen on the floor. He darted out to grab it and…

...CRASH!

He collided with Brother Pascual
and his big tray of seasonings.

Almonds, onions, and sesame
seeds sailed through the air.
Chocolate, chilies, and cumin
soared across the big room.
Garlic, peanuts, raisins,
and pimentos scattered to
the floor. Cinnamon, cilantro,
and salt floated overhead.

Plink! Plip! Plop! All the spices landed in the
pot where the turkeys were cooking.

"*¡Dios mio!*" cried Brother Pascual.
He fell to his knees and began to pray
with all of his strength.

The bells rang twelve times. The brothers
hung their heads. They had nothing to
feed the Viceroy. The meal was ruined.

Carlos felt a lump in his throat.
He had spoiled their chance to
find favor with the king.
What terrible trouble
he would be in!
Now the brothers would
give him nothing to eat.

But just then the most delicious smells began to rise from the simmering stew—a rich mixture of chilies, garlic, chocolate, and cinnamon. None of the brothers had ever smelled anything like it. Carlos just had to taste it.

"Get away from that pot," the brothers scolded. "Haven't you caused enough trouble for one day?"

"Ummm! *¡Rico!*"

"*¿Rico?* Really?"
The brothers gathered
to taste the sauce.

"*¡Que sabroso!*"
"*¡Delicioso!*"
"*¡Rico!*"
"Brother Pascual,
please, try it."

Trembling, they carried the stew to the dining room where the Viceroy waited.

"What a wonderful smell!"
said the Viceroy as he
prepared to take a bite.

The brothers held their breath
and waited.

The Viceroy tasted the dish. "How unusual!
This is the best dish I have ever tasted!
I give the cook my highest praise."

Brother Pascual bowed modestly. "In truth,
your honor, I do not deserve your praise.
All praise belongs to Him above."

Up above in the rafters, Carlos was glad to be out of trouble. He ate until he could eat no more. After all, the meal was *un puro milagro*, a complete miracle. He could not count on such luck every day.

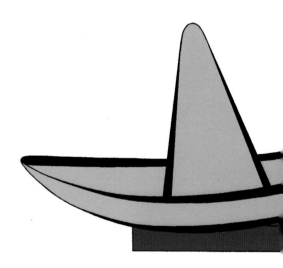

Author's Note

Molé is a thick savory sauce containing chocolate that is served over turkey or chicken. Known for the complexity of its preparation (it often contains as many as thirty-five ingredients), molé is prepared in Mexico for special feast days such as weddings and baptisms. The word *molé* comes from the Aztec word for sauce, which is "molli."

Though the dish probably originated with the Aztecs, the two most prominent legends give credit to the Spanish colonial convents and monasteries. One legend credits Sister Andrea of the convent of Santa Rosa. The other legend credits Brother Pascual Bailon. In both legends, the cooks were preparing a special dish for a visit from a Spanish Viceroy. Today, cooks from the region of Puebla still sing to Brother Pascual when they light their stoves in the morning:

San Pascual Bailon,
atiza mi fogon.

Saint Pascual Bailon,
help me to light my oven.

I first learned of the legend at an exhibit of Mexican folk art at the Crocker Art Museum in Sacramento, California. An ornate ceramic tree of life illustrated the story of Brother Pascual slipping and spilling the ingredients into one pot. I have taken the storyteller's liberty of adding the character of Carlos in order to capture a child's perspective.

Sources

Barros, Cristina and Buenrostro, Marco.
"Aclaran Mitos en Torno a la Creacion del Mole." 2003
http://www.cnca.gob.mx/cnca/nuevo/diarias/100699/mole.html.

"Cocina Mexicana: El Mole" 2003.
http://cocinamexicana.com.mx/historia/Mole.html

Gonzalez, Elaine. "Chocolate Legacy" Sept. 4, 2003.
http://www.chocolate-artistry.com/legacy.php.

"La Pagina de la Salsa Mole: Where is Mole From?" Sept. 4, 2003.
http://www.ramekins.com/mole/wheremole.html.

Mexican Folk Art Exhibit, Crocker Art Museum, Sacramento, California, 2003.

Palazuelos, Susanna. *Mexico: The Beautiful Cookbook*. San Francisco: Collins Publishers, 1994.